Animal Tricks:
Sticking Power

Written by Samantha Montgomerie

Collins

Staying safe is hard for animals.
They must look for safe spots.

Some animals can stick to things to keep them safe!

Staying stuck

The grey foot of the limpet helps it stay safe.

limpet

foot

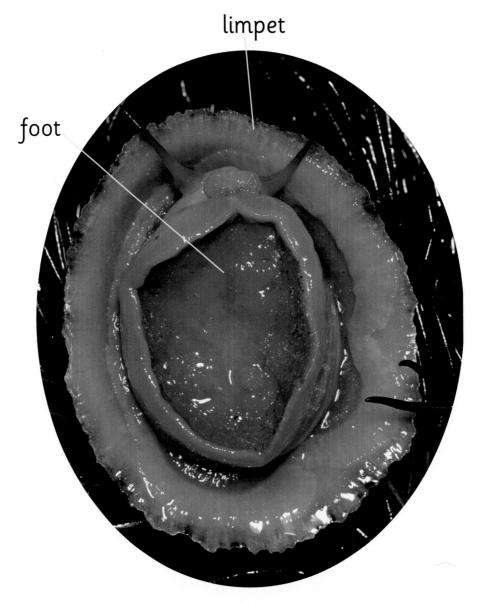

The waves cannot sweep it away from the rock.

Remora fish have sucker pads.
They can stick on to big rays
and sharks.

This remora gets a free lift
as the ray swims away.

Remora have the name
"sharksucker", too!

On the go

A trail helps snails stick
as they slither up
and along.

Snails make their way to food
and shelter high up.

Tree frogs have pads on their feet.
They stick as the tree sways.

The pads stop them dropping off.
They stay safe on the go.

Getting prey

Lizards grab prey with their thick spit.

When the lizard sees its prey … flick!
The prey stays stuck to the gloop.

Squid have long arms to grab prey.
Their suckers stick to it.

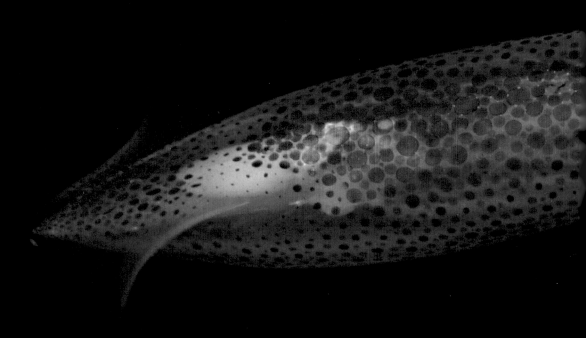

They grip the prey tight so it will not get away.

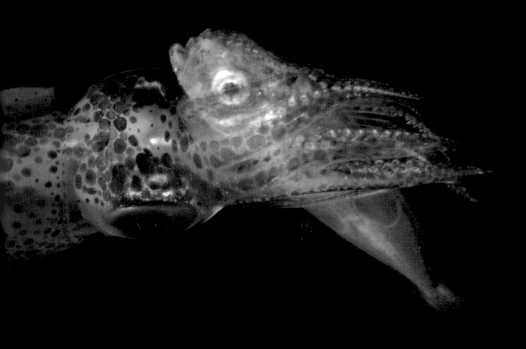

Staying safe

This eel digs a little cave in the sand.

Gloop from its tail makes the cave strong and safe.

The hagfish makes lots of gloop. This stops attackers killing it.

The attackers get the gloop and
the hagfish escapes!

Sticking helps animals to hunt, stay safe, flee or stay still.

With gloop, spit, fins or feet, animals have lots of tricks to stick.

Tricks to stick

Staying stuck

On the go

Getting prey

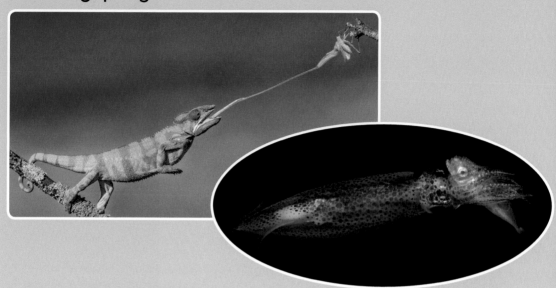

Staying safe

After reading

Letters and Sounds: Phase 5

Word count: 248

Focus phonemes: /ai/ ay, ey, a-e

Common exception words: of, to, the, have, their, when, little, some, go

Curriculum links: Science: Animals, including humans

National Curriculum learning objectives: Reading/word reading: read accurately by blending sounds in unfamiliar words containing GPCs that have been taught; read words containing taught GPCs; Reading/comprehension: understand both the books they can already read accurately and fluently and those they listen to by checking that the text makes sense to them as they read, and correcting inaccurate reading

Developing fluency

- Take turns to read a page of text, with your child reading the right-hand pages. Use a narrator's formal tone, checking your child uses a surprised or excited tone for the sentences that end with exclamation marks. If your child stumbles over a sentence, suggest they reread it again expressively.

Phonic practice

- Challenge your child to find words with different spellings of the /ai/ sound.
  - On page 5, ask: Can you find the word where the /ai/ sound is spelt a-e? (**waves**) Can you find a word where the /ai/ sound is spelt differently? (ay – **away**)
  - On page 11, challenge your child to find three words with different spellings of the /ai/ sound. (ey – **they**; ay – **stay**; a-e – **safe**)
  - Look through the rest of the pages, taking turns to find words with the /ai/ sound and identifying the spellings.

Extending vocabulary

- Look at page 2 and point to the word **hard**. Ask: Can you think of a word or phrase with a similar meaning (synonym)? (e.g. *difficult, awkward*)
- Repeat for the following:
  - page 2 **spots** (e.g. *locations, places*)
  - page 5 **sweep** (e.g. *wash, flush, push*)
  - page 10 **sways** (e.g. *moves from side to side, swings*)